HOW TO TRAIN
YOUR VIRGIN

NEW LOVERS is a series devoted to
publishing new works of erotica
that explore the complexities
bedevilling contemporary
life, culture, and
art today.

OTHER TITLES IN THE SERIES
We Love Lucy
God, I Don't Even Know Your Name

HOW TO TRAIN YOUR VIRGIN

×

WEDNESDAY BLACK

BADLANDS UNLIMITED
NEW LOVERS
Nº1

How To Train Your Virgin
by Wednesday Black

New Lovers No.1

Published by:
Badlands Unlimited
P.O. Box 320310
Brooklyn, NY 11232
Tel: +1 718 788 6668
operator@badlandsunlimited.com
www.badlandsunlimited.com

Series editors: Paul Chan, Ian Cheng, Micaela Durand, Matthew So
Consulting editor: Karen Marta
Copy editor: Charlotte Carter
Editorial assistant: Jessica Jackson
Ebook designer: Ian Cheng
Front cover design by Kobi Benzari
Endpaper art by Paul Chan
Special thanks to Luke Brown, Alex Galan, Martha Fleming-Ives, Elisa
Leshowitz, Marlo Poras, Cassie Raihl, David Torrone

Paper book distributed in the Americas by:
ARTBOOK | D.A.P. USA
155 6th Avenue, 2nd Floor
New York, NY 10013
Tel. +1 800 338 BOOK
www.artbook.com

Paper book distributed in Europe by:
Buchhandlung Walther König
Ehrenstrasse 4
50672 Köln
www.buchhandlung-walther-koenig.de

Printed in the United States of America

ISBN: 978-1-936440-80-1
E-Book ISBN: 978-1-936440-81-8

www.badlandsunlimited.com

For the Black Prince, and his baying hounds, too.
May the good chase never end.

CONTENTS

Prologue

He has found another one. I can see it in his eyes. Beside me at the table, before our guests, my king is all attention and husbandly devotion. But I can see *her* in his amber eyes—someone else, someone not me.

In the Onyx Hall our glittering guests titter and play as they await the arrival of dinner. They are rowdy tonight, these members of court, some antlered or furred, others hoofed and be-snouted, seizing the wine proffered by the cloaked servants as fast as it comes.

In the center of the hall a troupe of musicians pluck their fleshy instruments, the cartilaginous extrusions from their caved-in bellies thrumming to a familiar tune. A river of entertainers flows this evening, an opened vein of life in honor of my husband and me. Their music echoes among the buttresses of the Hall's ceiling, and dies in the tapestried dimness beyond our tables where the servants come and go. Already we have seen a merman and a mermaid making love in a clear vat, sinuous forms fucking among their cloud of bubbles, crying out in watery silence and release.

Yes, it is a hell of an affair, this

anniversary of ours. No one remembers the number anymore, or whether there was a first. For you see, time moves differently in my Realm than in yours. Here it spirals and warps, stutters and starts. And for the first time in this quaking eternity, I sense that this anniversary could be our very last. Something must be done.

There was a time when my king thought of me before any other, when thinking of me was what hardened that instrument, that bold cock. There was a time when he thought only of taking me from behind as hard and fast as he could, as if by plunging deep enough, long enough, he could fuck his way into my soul. I love him with that painful, yearning kind of love that invades the body from some other place—could it be the soul?—and can only be satisfied by the act of sex. Back then, when he had me under his control, hands on my ass, fingers pressing into my flesh, I felt his love and I was happy. But these days he is distracted by *her*, by *her*, and her and her and *her*—by the great panoply of lovely creatures walking the earth.

One of my king's messengers trots up to our table, a black dog who sits upon the sparkling carpet. I know it brings news of his latest love interest—a creature of your world. In its eyes I can see her face. Indeed my husband's messengers are not great concealers of secrets. And yet my husband does not suspect I can understand their communications. Like all husbands, he underestimates his wife.

As the servants deliver the feast, steaming boar with a single apple-sized cherry in its crisped snout, I study the human's image in the dog's eye. A girl young and fresh, with wide, Slavic cheekbones and short-cropped hair. A human pixie—but appealing to my husband and king where no true pixie could. Unlike us, she has the capacity for innocence. She is a virgin, doomed to age and wither, yes, but fresh in youth like newly fallen snow. The only kind he likes.

I smile at my guests. Why must I now be quarantined from his desires? Because he no longer loves me—not as he did? There was a time when we would seduce such a girl into our vast bed, when we would torture her untried, narrow cunt for days on end, sucking the honey from her slight thighs and rounded ass, before turning her onto her belly and fucking her to near death. My king with his cock and me with my tongue, no match for his hardness, no, but possessing a serpentine flexibility. My king used to make me proud: There was a malevolence about the way he would unsheathe that cock before the frightened creature, the way he would advance upon her despite her crying, her sudden change of heart, her protests. We were like two wildcats playing with supper—a team—and always with hearts and minds only for each other.

I want to crush those humans, those high-assed youths of whatever sex that take his attention and draw him away from me now. I want him under my thrall again, in love, at once in charge of my body, my breasts, my heaving cunt, and at my side always.

If I could send a shadow minion to take this new distraction screaming out of her human sleep—to push its long fingers up into her tight asshole and then to fuck her virgin pussy with its branched, terrible cock—to denude her of that alabaster virginity—well, I certainly would. Wouldn't you? But alas, that's not how it works.

There is a flourish of applause and catcalls as the guests celebrate the conclusion of the performance (a set of centaurs in heat). Now a dozen wood people have gathered in the open space. A single deep drumbeat smashes through the hall. A sudden hush falls as a vine girl steps forward, her fingers rustling with new leaves.

A sparrow, yet another of my husband's messengers, alights on the banquet table on the far side of him, beside the dog. I glance that way casually. Its eyes hold yet another ill-disguised vision of yet another human. I can feel my husband's ancient heart thump when he sees it. This human is similar to the other— can it be? Oh, my damn husband. It is a young man, his shoulders those of a man but his face lacking the crags and hardness of one. His eyes the same haunting, cloudy green as hers.

Two to ruin, then. I will coax from each of them that which makes them desirable to my king, that gentle, burgeoning sexuality. I will bring them to me through their dreams. I will seduce them into an initial depravity that will extinguish all innocence.

I raise my crystal glass and smile at my handsome husband.

"To you, my love," I say. "Forever."

"And to you," he says, raising his glass with his right hand and flicking away the bird with his left. We drink to our marriage, our eternal bond. He leans for a kiss, not knowing what I know. His crown shimmers.

"Our desire is undiminished after all these years," I say, and I reach beneath the table. My hand finds the place where his legs meet. Beneath the fabric his cock lies like a sleeping giant. Yet it is only a moment's work to free it. Without leaning over I unlace his ties, and, already awoken in so short a time, this beloved toy of mine bobs up against my hand.

My husband's eyes glint as if mined with shards of glass. My core twinges. I am immediately wet through with readiness for those lips, that thrusting tongue. Remembering the human twins, I flinch. In anger I clutch his cock and twist it. His mouth becomes a line as he rears away to peer down at me, perplexed. I continue to hold his cock, leaning now to keep it in hand as he strains away. My cunt is pulsing, but tears are forming in my eyes.

The music of the performance rises at that moment—an insistent drumbeat growing in volume. One of the vine men leads the vine girl forward. He is a hoary chap with face almost entirely occluded by the vines that grow from his skin. His body is shaggy with tendrils and leaves, and at his base, the thick genitals are petrified erect. His wooden feet clack on the mirrored tiles.

The diners have finished their meals.

The servants are slipping through the shadows, collecting their emptied plates or bringing lavish cakes and pies. More wine is poured. My husband reaches down and holds my hand on his cock, gently, as if to show me how. The vine woman is standing before us now, and the servants appear and disappear unbidden, clearing the table.

"A gift?" my husband asks me.

"Just like old times," I tell him.

The vine girl is a thing of beauty. Staggeringly lovely in the flawless way that all those who live in this realm can be whenever they wish. A willow tree made female flesh. It is this perfection that my husband has tired of, but it is all we have here.

Yet, although she is not human, my husband's cock obliges the gift: It grows

11

so that it touches the underside of the table. Beneath the girl's simple white shift her vines rustle and coil around the swell of her breasts. Her fingertips, themselves delicate twigs, begin to grow longer and thicken. She does not look us in the eye but gazes at the floor.

I remove my hand from my husband's cock and slip it down to my own lap, where my skirt, designed to split apart like tulip petals—my own design—falls open. I am hot, hot as sand in the sun.

The vine man begins to tear the woman's shift from her shoulders. One heavy breast is exposed, nipple dusky as bark, then the other. The vines ripple and flutter in the air.

"Let me," I say. The vine man backs away, bowing.

The guests are silent, leaning forward,

attentive. A few hands or paws have vanished into laps. Noble mouths hang open as secret contacts take place out of sight beneath the banquet tables. Rustling and snorting fill the air. I look around and smile. This is how it should be. All gazing at us, all feeling our energy, our heat. I reach forward and I tear the rest of the woman's dress away. She flinches. There she is. Naked, quivering, and filled with fear.

"On the table," I tell her.

She does not hesitate, though her eyes flick up at mine for an instant. She has heard about me. I am ripe with desire, knowing that she obeys my order even though she fears the outcome. This is where *my* desires lie—not with humans and their silly expiring bodies, their pains and passions and petty daily chores—

but with those that fear annihilation and yet consent anyway. The vine girl reclines on the table.

"Face me," I say. "Spread your legs."

And she spreads her legs to us, revealing her damp center, her ripe pussy lips beneath a smattering of soft hairs. My king and I stand now, looking at her. Beyond the table, the court looks back. Like a heartbeat the drum continues to throb. It is faster now. My cunt responds to the increased urgency: I squeeze myself and a thrill darts down each leg. Like the shifting, groaning guests, my husband is also open-mouthed. He is ready, with his pants now collapsing to the floor and his cock bobbing in the open air. Casting him a glance over my shoulder, I step forward and snatch a handful of her strange, sapling hair. I shake her.

"Wider."

Her pussy lips part to reveal a tiny slice of pinkness within. I lean in for the first taste, walking my fingers up her gleaming thighs as I do. Above her belly, her heavy breasts rise and fall with quick, shallow breaths. I flutter my tongue over her lower lips, easing them farther apart. She cries out once.

"Silence," I say, biting her wet center.

My husband grips me from behind. His cock rudely presses against my rear and his hands are already parting the skirts. Perhaps he loves me still. His bare skin and mine meet with an electricity that almost ruins everything—I almost explode at his touch, but I push back the release—I must wait, I must wait. He folds me at the waist, eager enough that my whole face is thrust roughly against the girl's pillowy, wet pussy lips. The hair there is softer than any human's, a downy corn silk, and I draw my long, deadly tongue up and down her from the lowest part to the apex of her clitoris, even as my husband positions himself at my entrance. Blood is pumping to my cunt; a twinge has rapidly become a constant agony. My mouth and nose are buried in the girl's shivering, shuddering depths. I can hear her crying out and I move my tongue faster. My husband butts his cock head against my entrance, forcing the broad, slick tip inside and pressing with a bruising power.

"Let me," he tilts upward, probing the opening for a weakness. "Let me in."

It's like a dark, secret cave in the vine woman's pussy. My husband adjusts the head of his cock until it is angled true, and with one push has it just inside. I squeeze him tightly and for a moment he laughs, for he can't enter farther. A game we play. How I love him! But he is strong and with a grunt he pushes past my defenses. The walls of my cunt are forced apart by his smooth cock. I groan into the girl's pulsing slit. She too is moaning loudly and I push my tongue even deeper, mimicking his cock, pressing up against her deepest spot again and again. I am a brutal tide.

"Oh, god," she screams.

"Take it, *you*," he orders.

I hear the guests—louder now, moaning, screaming even, but all I can see is her thighs on either side and her belly above. He is pumping me and my muscles are contracting around him, bruising themselves against his hardness. I'm quivering—a cannon is going off in my head and somehow he thrusts harder and harder and faster and faster despite my clenched muscles, deeper and deeper, and I moan out into the girl, vibrating my tongue so that a shudder starts in her thighs. She bucks all around me. The sound of her mingled pleasure and agony tips me over the scales, and everything contracts and swells and I am helpless, buried in this pussy but unable to do anything else. Filled from behind. Dominated entirely, my husband absorbed in me and our game, like the old times. I am loved.

And then my king pulls out of me without ceremony or kindness; my muscles clench together around his absence, and I gasp as he lifts me forward onto the girl, so that I am trapped face to face with her, sweat-slick breast to breast. Ribs clunk ribs. Eye to eye now, I see her pupils go wide.

"No!" I protest, pressing away from her face, from this proximity.

I feel him behind me and a vicious shame ignites where his cock was, where his love once was—as I realize what is happening. He is entering *her*—I can see it on her face— he is fucking *her* while I lie atop her like a beached sea creature, pinned in my humiliation by his weight.

"No, no!" I cry. And yet I am coming again—what has been started cannot be stopped now. I could slash his eyes out, rip out her tongue! He is going faster. The girl wails, weeps, shakes her head— her eyes roll back.

"Fucking wood beast, I'm going to

fill you up, little tree whore," he bellows over my shoulder. And he comes, exhaling into *my back,* in one long, shuddering gasp.

Quivering with my spent orgasm and hatred, I lie between them. I crane my head away from hers and look around at the Onyx Hall. The court guests are all around us, some so close that I could touch them where they stand. Farther off a number of guests are fucking, bent over tables or down on the stone floor. Tongues and tits and asses and cocks— lords and ladies, creatures of all kinds— performers become guests and guests, performers. They are smiling.

The king rolls his weight off me at last and I in turn roll off the girl with as much dignity as I can manage. I resolve to destroy her, to rip out her vine fingers—

but later. I have virgins to plot against now. My husband, spent, oblivious, has sat heavily and is drinking wine. His dog is whispering into his ear. I want to go to him, to scream in his face, why don't you want *me*?

But my legs buckle and servants are all around, bearing me to bed, away from the hall, away from my shame.

I

Planning the Successful Deflowering

At dawn the morning after, I am already working in the Baby Garden, the central sprawl of lawn, flowering trees, and shrubs girded by the Castle's living quarters on three sides, and on the fourth, by the archway leading to the grounds. From the windows the royal occupants can gaze down at the trees with their wriggling fruits—orbs made

up of curled fetuses of all species—
fairies and nixies and gnomes, winged
piglets, bearded dragons, toothpick-
horned unicorns. They hatch and uncoil
only when the Realm needs them, and I
am their mother. This morning I coax a
ripe flowering bush to release its infant
burdens. A whisper from me, a stroke of
my fingers, and down tumble the flower
babies, pale yellows and luminous greens,
arms and torsos like blades of grass, to
cavort on the obsidian flagstones. One
young fellow, amorous already, clasps
his slip arms around the middle of one of
his toddling partners and bends him (or
is it her?) over, preparing to penetrate.

The little victim screams joyous,
uncomprehending screams.

"Not yet, you," I say, separating them
and taking care not to tear their limbs.

"You have to wait until tonight."

These flower babies will have matured for tonight's entertainment, and by dawn they will be scattered across the mirrored tiles of the Onyx Hall like drying rushes, lifeless, to be swept by the hooded servants into the raging forever-fire in the great hearth. They live a single day, and spend most of it fucking one another in paroxysms of joy. I am hoping they will help the court forget my embarrassment.

"You will have your fill of love tonight, little ones," I say.

They gambol in the sunlight, graceful as sea grass, and make me believe that perhaps those new human interests of my husband are harmless dalliances after all.

It is lovely to think it. But then an

ancient voice and the scent of rocks long buried darken my garden. The flower babies shiver and pout, tripping over one another to hide in my skirts. I look to see what blocks the sun.

"My *Queen*."

The seer from the western bog. Her chin bulges and retracts, transparent and freckled.

"My Queen," she croaks.

"Yes, Bog Mother," I say, and I bow. Seers must be respected—even the vilest ones.

And she *is* vile. Already her filth has clouded the obsidian garden path. Her spores creep and rise in the air, seeking purchase. She is hugely pregnant; her thick dugs dangle to either side of the swollen belly. Her very skin is pimpled with the translucent eggs she will soon hatch. Inside, a thousand amphibious limbs twitch.

Whatever else she is growing, I don't care to investigate.

She curtsies, causing a loose egg to plop onto the tiles. The flower babies bury their petal faces in the grass, moaning in horror. Only one callow chap approaches the egg and pokes the gelatin exterior, staring back at the marble eye that appears within. His little cries are embarrassing, and with a flick of my tulip skirts I have blown the lot of them farther down the garden path.

"Have you noticed that your king's eyes wander as never before?" the Bog Mother rasps, her breath like slaughter, her eyes wicked and knowing. In them I see the sickness of her endless rutting, the fathers of her endless offspring flashing by—members of a thousand species. Even now there is probably something mating with her—a plant, an insect, something invisible and as vile as she is.

I snatch her right breast and twist it.

"Do you want to die, crone?" I hiss. "Keep your tongue inside!"

A rain of dislodged eggs splashes my feet. She winces but continues. "As a mother in the Realm, my sympathies are with my Queen. I am here only to warn you. Your king and husband's infidelities could destroy the realm itself. It is your love that makes our realm real. Your love for each other, and your passion, are the glue that binds our existence. You must not let him indulge himself. Not now. Not when the connections are weakening."

I release her breast and look away. I will not tell her I know only too well.

"Get out of my palace," I tell her, weary. "You've only come to gloat with the rest of them."

The old woman licks her lips.

"You must put an end to the threat, my Queen."

I kick her savagely, and she leaves in a trail of decaying eggs that will never now hatch. The flower babies are tugging at my robes, keening. This time it is *I* who has frightened them.

"Shhh," I tell them. "All will be well."

Of course, I know the Bog Mother is right. I must act immediately.

×

This is how it's done...

1: Know Your Virgin

As the orange suns climb the sky I wander out of the Castle to walk the border between our realms—where your dreams occur. My unknowing king slumbers off the night's revelries in our bower, snoring among the lilies that grow from our loamy bed, a cool breeze brushing aside the hairs from his big, handsome skull.

Out at the borders, your minds are even clearer to me.

And what's this? As I poke at the edges of the boy's and girl's unconscious mind, I begin to understand why my great horned husband, what with his many black dog accomplices and raven spies, has not yet moved on them to fuck and buck them into happy stupefaction. At first I believed that my husband wanted to draw out the conquest. But that is wrong. You see, his boy and girl? They are not easy marks, for all their sweet, plump lips and wide eyes. For one thing, they are in that sly, hipster stage, a recent development in human life spans that makes for grueling, unsatisfying seductions. Ask one and he'd say (the hipster in general, mind you) that he is too clever by far to succumb to romance, passion, *abandon*. The hipsters' seductions exist in a glare of technology and bloody-headedness that renders them, most of them, repulsive to my kind. They simply don't *believe*.

But these two delectables? These are harder marks *by far.*

Take the short-haired girl— *M*— her foreigner's name simplified because no one can pronounce it. Though she is slight through the waist and thighs, her full-blown womanhood is evident in her buoyant, round breasts. These she hides in heavy sweatshirts, but her long neck and her tapered fingers betray the grace and womanhood within. Her nose is slender but not small. It is a queen's nose. Beneath it the pronounced cupid's bow of her top lip bends in a constant frown, and even in sleep her dark eyebrows strain toward one another as if she is angry. When I try to enter her dreams I am stymied by tinctures for depression, anxiety, suffering. She is smothered by pharmaceuticals. There is nothing for a lady's claws to grip: M is a Teflon-coated soul. I look deeper into the swirling mist of her mind.

But what can such a girl have to be depressed about? Doesn't her beauty change with the day like a morning glory that never closes? At dawn she is elfin and by dusk she is a raving beauty of spilled onyx curls and gently bleeding mascara. In the rise and fall of her chest in sleep, the light outline of ribs beneath skin not abraded by life, I see only the sweetness of a fairytale maiden-fair.

There it is. I step back for a moment, shocked at what I have found. For M's past holds a darkness that would stun a sewer troll. I see screaming women, bombs, bullets, a baby tossed on a fire. I see now: M and Peter grew up *together* in another land—a war-torn wasteland of atrocity—from which they are now refugees. Thus the antidepressants, and perhaps, just perhaps, the tenacity to virginity.

M and Peter are simply too busy

surviving to dream *my* dreams. I withdraw from M and turn my attention to Peter. In the Real they live very close to one another, in adjacent buildings in a small town.

Peter's mind is different. Peter-of-the-hairs-curling-around-his-ears does not take pills of forgetfulness. No. He allows himself to be swallowed nightly by his memories. In Peter's dreams rockets crash, women shriek under the rapine attention of beings of clotted ash and fury. He is so crowded with bellicose monsters—great blustering beings from another realm where soot and industrial detritus hang in the air—that I can barely elbow in for a look at him. There's no room for my crystal step, my faint perfume, the susurrus of spring leaves.

Poor boy. Poor, poor boy. I walk in my gardens while I think, idly kicking the verminous grass sprites out of my flowers as I go.

So. M and Peter's trauma explains why my king has not succeeded. But he is not in a rush, and I am. I glance up at the castle to our bedroom balcony. The afternoon breezes blow the crimson curtains out like angel wings. I see a trail of thread where they are fraying. Already it is happening, then: the disintegration of my Realm and the bleed-out of my power.

I snap my fingers as I get an idea. The trees stand a little straighter, the flowers bloom a little wider. I will not *just* take their virginities. I will instruct them in my dark techniques and then, when they fairly burst with my influence, my dripping divinity of sex, I shall present them to him as if they were twin hunting dogs. Maybe I'll have them eating from my hands, one on each side. Or maybe lapping at my cunt adoringly.

Get a load of these two, *hubby*.

That is, I believe, the way *your* people would put it.

×

2: Approaching Your Virgin

Tonight, as planned, I am at table with my husband and court, the orgy-prone flower babies parading before us to a divine musician whose instrument is his long, vibrating, and cat-gut-threaded penis.

"A wonderful celebration, my love," says my husband. I look for his black dogs and ravens but I see none. They must be busy seeking a way in, just as I am. I call impatiently for more wine.

"Drink, my King," I order, and he drinks. In some things he still obeys his Queen.

When at last I steal away, holding my skirts up as I approach the grey border between realms, it is late. In peering into your world I stop.

"Wonderful!" I whisper. The Real has done me a favor! With all its microbes and such. It has given Peter a flu-like illness! He is sunk beneath a gauze of medicines brought by a tiptoeing, sweet-faced M, and his sleep is oddly free.

Thank the Real for nighttime cold-and-cough syrup, for it opens a path through Peter's shattered dreamscape wide enough for one small queen.

×

I tiptoe that path through his shattered interior landscape: sneaking into Peter's mind as gently as I am able. Over the scarred, silent battlegrounds of his mind I travel, ever faster. I pass a sunny beach where infant Peter splashes in the surf, a cloth diaper sagging on his little loins. I pass a birthday party in a tent, toddler Peter in a clown nose and freckles, mouth ringed with cake frosting. Then I pass a farm, where gangly Peter in rubber boots slogs with a pale of milk among indifferent heifers. I pass many memories in Peter's mind, and always I see Peter growing taller, the man's jaw emerging in his youthful face. Eventually I gain speed: after all, I don't have all night. I hurry toward a raging light in the distance, and there I find a collapsing house. I stop to look. Yes. Peter is here, now, dreaming. Through a cracked window I see him as he sees himself right now: a tiny curly-haired boy huddled near a bled-out woman. Peter dreams he is little boy Peter.

"Mama," he calls, weeping.

I have no time for this—I've got another innocent to fuck before the night is through. Oh, I know I sound cold. Peter's suffering is heartbreaking if you are susceptible to that sort of thing, that is to say, if you have a heart. But I've not had a heart, that kind of heart, for eons. It's possible I never did. And this quivering boy will simply not do. I need a strapping man, not a shivering heap.

I enter the room as naked as a

dream of a naked woman—which is a very different thing from a real naked woman, you must know: I am perfect as no human woman could be—perfect in that way that men, human men, really want women to be. I am all things. My skin is delicate and pliable, yet firm. I am hard, yet yielding. I am round in the dark and flat in the light. I am flat in the light and round in the dark. My nipples glow in rosy warmth and then give way to tawny tightness, as if chilled by bathing in a blue sea. The hairs at my cunt are present but not intrusive, hiding the treasures but not *impeding* them. My dark interior forest inciting, not frightening. I cast a golden light across the shadowy space. I can change from the Venus of Willendorf to the androgynous Athena—I come as they wish and change as they will.

So. I become the angel of deliverance that he needs right now. An angel he can *fuck*.

Sure enough, when Peter sees me he winks out of my sight and then back again—from boy to man. In his proper form, his man's eyes take me in with hunger. I reach for him.

"You must come with me now," I say. I gesture at his motionless mother, and as I do I erase some of the blood that has pooled around her, the soldiers' boot prints all around. "Take my hand."

He looks again at the body. It is an act of great magic even for me to prevent her blood from filling the dream room again, so strong is Peter's grief.

"She is out of her pain," I soothe. "You must come. You must experience life and pleasure. She would want it." I grip his fingers in mine.

After a time the boy/man nods and wipes his lovely nose on the back of his hand and comes to me. I wrap him in my diaphanous robes and press him between my bare breasts. As his firm body molds with mine in an embrace, a bead of pleasure trickles through my loins. He moves his strong arms around me and his proximity sends a green shoot of pleasure to my breasts. Just as I start to gloat—*ah, success*—he speaks out loud.

"Mama," he says.

"Oh, no. Not *me*," I growl, pulling away from him. This won't do at all. We can't stand here and reenact his mommy issues on the killing floor!

So I take him away...

✕

(Here I must interrupt with a brief note about seducing virgins. In seducing a human virgin, especially a shell-shocked, internally wounded human virgin, setting is of paramount importance. It is everything. The precise arrangement of objects, of light, of scenery and story, is critical to a successful seduction. But you must be clever and resourceful. Each virgin is different, after all. Each requires a different key to unlock his or her consent. Alas, gone are the golden, simpler days of Victorian canoes and straw hats with little ribbons around them; of shady picnics in fields of flowers; of wine and roses.

Today, you have to get *creative*.)

×

3: Proper Training Environment

A police hovercraft races overhead, blowing the boy's hair from his face. (I watch from afar as he finds himself in this new space.) He looks down to discover his clothing: cargo pants and military boots tied high on his calves, a black T-shirt and leather trench coat, a gun holster at hip, thigh, and back. Where is he? He feels a sense of freedom, suddenly, and he whoops.

"Get down!" screams a girl.

He whirls to look at her. It is only when the blimp advertising some kind of Korean face cream looms overhead, drawing his attention to the landscape of teeming high-rises, bristling antennae, searchlights, and swarming hovervehicles, that he is able to look away from her. (I'm quite proud of this temptress, having modeled her after half a dozen previous victims. She is pert and athletic-bodied, the kind of sprite whose unostentatious sex-appeal makes her accessible to young men frightened of women—which is all of them, mind you.)

"Get down!"

"For what?" he says. His heart is pounding through his T-shirt. Off he goes, his eyes locked on the girl's high, tight ass in her full-body black-something-or-other suit.

"Quick! Follow me!" she says. She has a wicked-looking gun on her thigh.

Two huge air-cycles bump and skid onto the rooftop behind them. Enormous men kick-stand them and charge toward Peter, snorting and grunting.

"You! Stop!" one shouts, guttural as a boar. The threat of violence in the voice startles Peter. (My pig men, of course, in full

dream-mufti).

The bullets come soon after they do, whacking into the rooftop around him. He skitters to the right, then the left, then takes off after the girl.

"Wait!" he cries.

"Run!" she commands, pistoning over the rooftop.

They drop through a hatch and sprint down a corridor lit by bare bulbs. He can hear the big men gaining, their footfalls shaking the hallway, and when he turns he thinks he sees a flash of tusk. He trips and falls. They are upon him.

"Got you, pretty boy."

"Let's work him over."

Peter is on his hands and knees but they quickly knock him to his stomach.

"Get down!" they shout.

"You thought you could get away with

it, did you?"

"I didn't do anything!"

"Shut up and stop moving," says the bigger one. (Snoar, the pig man.)

"Let's show him what we do to pretty boys," says the other (My good pig man, Sny).

They switchblade his belt off and work the pants down around his knees. Peter is a strong man in the Real, an athlete, but now he finds himself weak as a paper doll. They've gotten his pants down and he feels their hot breath on his shoulders (I make sure he does), and now they are fumbling with his underwear and denting the skin of his ass with their fingertips and he cries out in shame. He has always wanted to test himself with men, he thinks, but not like this. (What a surprise, to learn this!)

"Damn you," he howls in his native language.

"Get ready," laughs Snoar, applying a fingertip to his mouth, slathering it with saliva, and then fumbling around Peter's buttocks.

Peter squeezes his eyes shut as he feels that man's large, moist finger probe closer.

"Oh, god," he thinks as the tip of the finger presses his anus. He clenches himself to prevent its penetrating. (Snoar can go no farther than he is permitted; he cannot take Peter against his will—as much as he wants to—just as I cannot. The trick is that Peter does not know this. He feels only the terrible pressure of the probing, cigar-thick finger.)

"Ready?" repeats Snoar.

"Set," says Sny. (To make sure our trembling hero gets the full effect of my fantastic show, I rend the dream fabric so

that the boy can actually see *Sny digging his long, curved cock out of his pants; see Snoar remove his finger from Peter's cleft and start to free his own cock. Released, it hovers over Peter's bare backside like a torpedo, and the boy struggles again.)*

"Go," shouts a female voice, followed by two blasts of gunfire.

Bullet casings tinkle on the earth on either side of Peter's face and the attackers slump and die above him in fountains of theatrically steaming blood.

×

4: The Art of Seduction

"They were going to…" Peter says, angrily pacing the basement hideout, slamming his fists into the pipes and shaking the space. A realistic room, if I do say so myself. "I should have killed them myself."

"I wouldn't have let them do anything," she says/I say. I have taken over the form of Peter's timely savior and left him to his private thoughts, the better to focus on the proceedings-to-come. It is messy in these heads of yours, among the turbulent neuron currents.

"I would have found a way to kill them," he says. "They can't do things like that to people."

I am struck by his fury. I had thought him a broken man by the look of his war dreams, but his eyes are full of strength and defiance now. The forced deviation from his usual dreams is doing him good, and perhaps this seduction will turn out to be fun. Before his eyes I shed the skintight uniform, revealing small budding breasts, long limbs, an already swelling pussy with the faintest womanly wisp of hair at the top. He gapes at me.

"You know, there aren't a lot of real men left in this world," I say, gesturing to the low ceiling and the dystopian metropolis far above.

"You're beautiful," he says.

He watches me as I start a slow dance around the room. I touch myself with two fingers, holding my other hand aloft in the dance. I eye the creature at his groin and rub my center, my clitoris springing forward out of its hood like the center of an orchid, inflamed with color and vibrance. His eyes grow larger. I am wet. I sway to him and place my glistening fingertips at his mouth to introduce him to the taste of me. He takes my fingertips in his mouth and he sucks them. Tears form at the corners of his eyes.

I find myself feeling guilty, thinking of all that I saw when I dipped into his mind moments ago—all that he has suffered.

"I want to feel you," I tell him, not adding what I *really* want to say: "Fuck me until I can feel something good again."

He holds me on either side of my hips, leaning down to seek my lips with his. They are warm and soft and I am bent back under their urgency. Then he falls to his knees and buries his face in my cunt. His lips are hesitant—he does not know what to do—he starts to lick the space just above my clitoris. I press his scalp with gentle fingertips, guiding him lower to the heart of my pleasure, and his warm tongue flicks and probes.

He is untrained, I have seen this much, but because of his eagerness, his gratitude, he is doing everything right. His hands slide down my hips and up again. The tremor of happiness at being touched like this is almost enough to make me weep. Now it is my turn to be grateful and I arch over him, letting my hair curtain his broad, smooth back. I have not been touched with love for so long.

Only with efficiency.

I gasp.

He stops and looks up at me as my body continues up the gentle slope of pleasure. I am already starting to come, in slow, rolling waves, like a ship glimpsed in the distance across a stormy sea. It will not be long now.

"You're crying," he says. His voice is worried.

"I'm not," I say, and I make it so. I am not crying in this dream.

He stands, dragging those long fingers up my borrowed-persona's skin, until he comes to my breasts. He touches them, pinching the nipples just a little until I throw my head back and moan. And then that warm mouth is on my breast, gently questing, circling each in turn.

His fingers find my cunt again and explore the opening. I twitch.

"Please," I say.

He holds my hands. Is it he who is trembling, or I? He seems so assured now. He guides me to the bed. I can see the hard line of his cock through his underwear, upright and ready. He will need so little training, this one. I recline on the bed, with him arranging the sheets and pillows around me like the most careful of servants.

He fixes me with his deep green eyes.

"I love you," he says, and I force back a bitter laugh. He is only a dreaming boy, after all. For who can love so quickly—quickly as lightening fire flashes and dies in the forest—but an innocent *innocently dreaming*? That innocence will be nothing but a memory soon.

I ruffle his hair and lean back, luxuriating in the moment, in the pulse and pressure in my cunt. If he touches me I might explode, might wipe us both out with my release, my throbbing completion. I smile at him and shake my head. He has no idea how much power I conceal.

He starts to work down his underwear, his eyes on my languishing body the whole time. His cock springs free. "I love you," he insists, capturing it in one hand, proudly.

×

(A word about humans. Humans are dumb. Really. They are very silly. They don't realize that their dreams are as real as their Real. They don't understand the consequences of anything. And they use this word *love*. You should always avoid using this word if you can. It brings nothing but destruction. I should know. I was alive when your kind was still dragging rocks around to make henges, when ten sticks in a circle would have done the time-keeping trick just as well.)

×

I cannot look at his big, wet eyes anymore. It is too painful, seeing a desire there that I once saw in my own husband and king. I focus on his glossy cock instead and I feign anxiety.

"Will it fit?"

×

(Another thought on virginity. The best way to train a virgin is to masquerade as a virgin yourself, even if you are the farthest conceivable thing from a virgin, and have been so since the seas covered everything and the most intelligent thing on the planet was a jelly-*thing* that didn't even have a brain.)

×

He rubs it down to the shaft and up to the head where a bead of precum sparkles.

I lean in to kiss my own brine from his lips and he engages with me, deeply. He holds my head, guiding my neck to tilt with his. Then he pushes me down with great strength and urgency, settling on top of me and between my legs, pushing them apart and up so that I am nearly folded in half. He hulks over me, kissing me again, so deeply I am glad I don't need to breathe like humans. I want him deep inside.

But why move so fast? I must not allow his first conquest to go too quickly— that would not be good instruction on my part, and I ease to the edge of the bed, despite his protestations, his urgent hands. I must make it great for the art of it, for the heat, for the accomplishment and the bloody victory over my damn, roving husband. I conjure for us candlelight, spiced air, and fresh rain to tickle the windows. I draw him to the edge so that his legs are dangling down, and then I kneel before him, before the scepter of young, untried sex filled with the blood of dreams. He is large, firm, thick, but not oversized. He will make a lot of women happy someday, if we can just cure him of his night terrors. If I train him he will be a boon to the women of your world. He will know how to please them, to be unselfish, and to take nothing for himself. I must be careful, now that I have him. I can take my time. I show him my center and rub my fingers along it, circles that make me moan. I am not acting. I want him to see how he can please a woman without even entering her, if need be. And that this is the unselfish way to be. I stroke myself, reaching out to muss his hair now and then, and his hands rub my breasts and he breathes louder and louder.

I *want* to curl myself against his broad young chest, to feel his human heat warm my ancient being, to bask in that folly, that love, and make it my own for a short time. I want to feel him enter me, part my lips with his thickness and drive home into my belly the meaning of that word *love*.

I mean this man-child no real harm, do I?

I only want to save my Realm. My King.

Then I go to him. I look up at him, drawing my fingers across his testicles, the rise of them, almost hairless, the flesh perfect. Above them his penis rises proud, nonvirginal, direct and desirous. I place my tongue there and begin to draw the tacky liquid between us like a spider draws its thread. He inhales and I climb atop him, positioning his thick, slick cock head at my entrance. The head starts to kiss my entrance when—

He shifts. I feel it. Not his body—his dream *body* is still there—but something in his dream *mind* has shifted. His face is blank. Blank. His eyes have gone dull and distant.

Somewhere, far in the distant war-torn world, the engines of war are roaring to life. An aircraft howls overhead, shaking the lover's nook, spilling plaster in my hair. And suddenly we are back in the war house. The walls tremble with dropped artillery and exploding shells. I hold him tightly, for he is mine. I have won him! I have won his love and I must make him mine now, before my husband steals it from me and I lose everything. Everything.

"Don't let it take you," I whisper to him, right into his face and his distant, already gone eyes. "Don't leave what we have found here in this safe place."

"Mama," he whispers, his eyes elsewhere.

So. He is already gone.

I have lost him.

II

Adjusting Your Training Methods

My realm stretches in all directions until it meets itself again (something your paltry human mind only *thinks* it can imagine). All is silent in the Castle when I return, although the day is still rich with light.

I enter the silent Onyx Hall. The gentle sighs of changeling-babes, those stolen humans whom we fit with pale leather wings and balsa lyres, echo among the buttresses far above, lost in shadow and not singing, but dreaming of singing, perhaps, as they float. Perhaps they are dreaming of their mothers from long ago. At least here they will never grow old. Here nothing does. Or nothing should. For there is a whiff of mildew in the air, as if decrepitude had passed through already.

My robes drag behind me like lifeless wings. Servants materialize and follow, lifting my train as I ascend the stairs to my bedchamber. There he is, my deplorable husband, abed still, deep in the state we call *obliva*. Dismissing the servants, I recline beside him. Combing his beard with my fingertips, I dip into his *obliva* and see the boy, Peter—a fantasy Peter. He is naked and kneeling before my husband. Fantasy Peter is stroking my husband's cock with a tongue like velvet. My husband's eyes are rolled back and his head is bent forward on his massive chest. It is as if he is trying to suck the boy's innocence and freshness into himself.

I choke my bitterness down. Why has my husband tired of me? Of our Realm? What can he find in these disposable human youths? I walk the Castle, thinking.

×

In a dark corner of the lower level, where the doorways lead to the Underworld, I detect the sounds of struggle and illicit passion. A stifled cry, a low groan. Curious, I creep toward it, trailing my fingertips across the dank walls to where two corridors meet.

It is the ghost woman, her full breasts shining now, her athlete's body Amazonian in its hardness. In the torch light the whiskers of her leopard's head are like filaments of pure light. She is on hands and knees. Towering over her, front hooves set beside each sinewy arm, is the centaur. She turns those lovely, expressionless eyes on me, her feline nostrils moist. In its inexorable plunge the centaur's groin slaps the perfect curve of her ass. I feel in myself a spark of interest, a trickle of wet between my legs. I long to be taken, tamed, appropriated, as this centaur is lording over this ghost woman. A current of golden electricity in my center compels me to walk forward.

I smile, giving them my blessing to

go on, and I join them.

"You do us great honor, my Queen," grunts the centaur. Centaurs are focused creatures, being made of the stallion's lust and the man's intelligence and deliberation. His back hooves scrape over the stones with the force of his movement, to hold him steady against the ghost woman's receptive gyrations.

I brush aside my robes and I float. When I am close I lean toward the centaur's strong, cruel mouth, and his arms enfold me even as he gives his bulk to the ghost woman. His heat penetrates my frozen interior, my sadness, and I lean against him, moved with each powerful thrust.

I run my hand from his back down to where the flesh meets the horse's coat. He closes his eyes in pleasure. Beneath him the ghost woman has started to push back against him with quiet insistency. The thrusting grows faster and I wrap my legs around his neck to better cling with him against this tide. The ghost woman moans and wails, and then shudders violently.

"Good girl," I whisper. "Now," I say to the centaur, "isn't it the Queen's turn?"

×

The centaur carefully detaches himself.

"Not here," I say.

Together we three navigate the dark passages to a still lower level of the Castle. From here I can hear the clanking of the Underworld.

"Here, my Queen?"

The centaur guides me into an empty chamber. Someone has been making this long-unused chamber a love nest, I see. Crimson and silver bedding has been draped carelessly over the old bed frame. A spent candle waits on the night stand beside a ewer encrusted with opals. So many secrets in my very own Realm.

"I want you to make me feel as you feel," I tell them.

I let them both guide me to the makeshift bed, her hands brushing back my long hair, his hands gently sinking me onto my hands and knees on the bed before him. I am something gentler than the ghost woman, if more powerful, but my interior trembles with anticipation of his large, mythic cock. Will I be able to take it without changing my form? I grit my teeth and raise my ass to him. Maybe I want to hurt. I want to be hurt. I want to feel something definite, something deep and penetrating. Something that will take me over, split me in half.

I want to feel anything but the pain of my husband's infidelity.

"I don't want to hurt you, Mistress," he says.

"I created you," I scoff. "Fuck me, please."

When he enters me the ghost woman nuzzles my neck, the silken fur and coolness of her nose a strange thing in the still gloom of the chamber. Suddenly I am pushed forward on the bedding a full three feet before she catches me and holds me in his path.

"Oh, gods."

I brace myself against her, opening

myself to this monster. He locates my ready cunt with his cock's head.

Fuck me, I think. *Fuck me until I can't think anymore.*

And then it happens. He punches through my powerful, clamping muscles until his entire length, the killing wholeness of it, lodges within. And then I am locked, secured to his powerful rhythm, and it seems that he has become one of Peter's vast war-machines, a pummeling, punishing being that wants only to take. His hands grip either side of my ass and he is large, yes, but I am a queen, and he is not *too* large, and for all his furious propulsion he is somehow gentle, considerate. I am not cored out by him, only *utterly explored* to my very center. Then he grows faster, and I come in shot-gun blasts of pleasure, one after the other after the other. His urgency slides both the ghost woman and me forward on the table—so strong is he.

"My Queen," he says, pushing harder. "Take all of me, my beautiful Queen."

"Kill me," I whisper. "Kill me with it."

But he cannot hear me over the sounds he is making in his massive equine lungs. She does though: The limpid-eyed ghost woman looks at me with infinite sympathy, and I cannot meet her gaze for long.

"I'm coming," he rumbles. "I'm coming in the Queen." And he increases his pace so that my breath catches in my throat and I can only hang on.

The ghost woman exhales in my ear. Her whiskers tickle my breasts as she laps a bead of sweat.

But I, I am thinking of the lovely

boy, Peter, and his poor gazelle-like companion, M. But pleasure floods my center and I gasp, long and hard, and behind me he pants and draws to his own conclusion, filling me with his warm seed.

And then his hooves slip a bit and he staggers, nearly punching right through me. He catches himself just as a ray of amber light pierces the darkness.

A corner of stone has crumbled, dislodged by his heavy hooves. Our three faces peer down into the flaming depths of the Underworld and its foundry. Sparks fly and hammers rise and fall in eternal toil. Beneath the foundry, invisible from here, is the dungeon.

And I get an idea.

×

1: Choosing the Right Moment

Two days later I am descending in a clanging iron elevator through the underworld with a small entourage of discreet servants. Around us workers churn the earth for the raw ore of this realm. I've been waiting for my opportunity these last days, and tonight it has come. For even though M is smothered by antidepressants and the like, she is also a user of Molly, an ecstasy-inducing drug that takes you humans right into my path. It coaxes the unconscious mind to show itself, much as a worm on a lake's surface will draw an ordinarily elusive fish. But these drugs do even more than that: They allow me to more deftly control the human's dreams.

I have brought my faithful minotaur, Freight; the vine girl, who owes me a favor after being party to my humiliation; Snoar and Sny, the pig men, and others—for atmosphere.

Level after level of sweating realm flesh, honed to fine musculature, rushes up and past us.

This time I can't fail. It is too perfect. And when she comes, we will be ready.

"Did you see any of my husband's black dogs? His ravens?"

Freight looks from beneath a heavy cowl. "We have seen his black dogs skulking around these last days, but we don't think they have detected this possible opening."

"Possible? It is failproof."

"Maybe, my Mistress. But they

haven't noticed it, or have deemed it unworthy."

"And Peter?"

"Untouched. The boy continues in his impenetrable nightmares."

"Good," I say.

The elevator continues to descend past a team of winged oxen attempting to drag some stubborn machine.

"Freight?"

"Yes, my Queen?"

"Why do men and women grow tired of what they once loved? Why must they lose interest?"

Freight knows of whom I am speaking—my own dear husband (and his king) who could crush him with the twitch of his antlered head—and he thinks long on his answer. At last: "In the many realms, my Queen, there are many wonders to know and many dangers to avoid. A man like the King is built with the hunger to discover which is which."

The elevator at last meets the nadir of its shaft. We have traveled beneath the mines and the foundry works where there is only a vast amphitheater laid out before us. Ringing it are the dungeon's oubliettes. At the center of the amphitheater a triad of sturdy posts has been arranged, and awaits our virgin. Torches flicker in a subterranean wind.

"Go on," I say. "Finish what you started saying."

"That is all, my Queen."

"Thank you, Freight." I nod. I trace the line of his muscular abdominals until they vanish beneath his breeches. It is a good enough answer and I will not kill him for his impudence. Not yet.

×

2: Obedience Training

M's cloudy-green eyes open into the dream we have built for her, yet something is wrong. Although her mind is open to me, the swan-necked girl does not have the fear I predicted when she discovers herself in a dank dungeon, roped to three upright posts. Furthermore, she is fighting mad.

But what a sight! Even your Tinkerbell could not look so innocent, nor wrestle so daintily with the fat ropes wrapped around her limbs. Her tiny waist looks like it might snap from the force of her struggles. Her short hair I have enhanced for the fantasy, and it now reaches her collarbone in dark, damp corkscrews. I stride forward with my favorite whip snaking behind me. This time there will be no mistakes. Her cheeks are pink with effort, her brows narrowed, her moist lips hang open as she breathes. I long to place my tongue between those lips, to drink her beauty and humanity into me. But this isn't a pleasure cruise.

"Welcome, you dear, pathetic little creature."

"Let me go," she snarls, glancing up briefly before returning to her rhythmic struggling. My minions Snoar and Sny sniff in her direction, snouts moist. Her nipples are so hard and sharp they could pierce the diaphanous shift that covers them.

"Don't bother, little Houdini." I laugh at her struggles. "There's no trick in the bonds, just good old-fashioned knots." M snorts in derision.

"What is this?" she spits.

"You know what I hate?" I remark, idly sliding on a pair of long, soft gloves made of whitest leather.

"I don't care what you hate. Let me go, you weirdo. You think you look *scary*?"

I carefully arrange the gloves over each fingertip as I think of how to proceed with this shrew. Perhaps the magic toadstools or mushrooms or whatever she takes works *too* well.

"No one house-trains these kids anymore. They just don't know how to show respect," I say. And then I release my tongue. Down it goes, inch by inch. Her eyes fix on it and stay, following its tip until it is inches from the stone floor. With it I can sense M's burgeoning youth, the tiny pulsing beacon of her untested cunt. Untested perhaps. But interested and awake. This won't be hard.

"What the fuck?" she says, wrenching her shoulders.

The clinking of the foundry workers far above drifts over us. The only other sound is her labored breathing.

"Exactly," I murmur.

Then? I whip her. I do. I am tired. I am angry at her beauty, her stubbornness. I am full of sadness. I whip her so that it *hurts,* and I do it with my tongue, not the whip. A red line stripes one smooth thigh, causing her to jump. Another razored lick and there is a twin to match it just above. I lash out yet again and open another wound across those two, creating a little box. *Wouldn't my husband be proud?* Three marks.

"Stop," she screams. Then she bites her tongue and glares at me.

Flick! I taste her blood, all metal and life. Snick! A stripe appears on her other thigh. Snick! A slice into the neat flesh over the bicep. Snick. Snick. Snick. I don't bother going into *her* head: *I know* it hurts.

I will make her trade her maidenhead to get out of this molten dungeon.

Drawn to watch the show are the other occupants of this deepest, dankest part of my Realm, mostly those cast out of the above when they are too sick or old or crazy. There have been more and more in recent times. I've never seen such a crowd. Where have they all come from? They gather at the boundary between torchlight and darkness. They scrabble on the tiles and they hiss and gobble and howl, a thousand beasts of scales and claws and withered limbs.

"Get her! Cut the pretty!" They bray. And much worse.

"You're a bitch," says M, blood coloring her exquisite lips.

I unleash everything. I slice her across that pretty face, those tender breasts, that secret garden of a pussy. The watchers titter and bay for blood. She does not scream.

"Freight!" I say.

Freight approaches. Ignoring her struggles, he traces her breasts beneath her shift. He is all man, my tall Freight. Her face is level with the chain-link geometry of his torso.

"Feast your eyes on that, little girl," I say.

She eyes me with hate as Freight slips his big fingers into her mouth. He holds them there when she tries to shake him away, probing deeper, and then he draws her bottom lip out. His cock is rising beneath his pants; she can see it as well as I can. Her eyes grow frantic as it rises. But in the dream logic she is also beginning to enjoy herself. I can smell it. Her arousal at Freight. Strange creatures, you humans. And it won't do. I'm not here to give her a picnic, a run-of-the-mill turn-on. I'm here to fuck her brains out. All I need is a whimper of consent.

"Behave," I tell her. "Or Freight will take you in that cell there, and he's going to lay you down on your back and he's going to spank you the only way he knows how."

Freight takes his crotch in one hand and rubs it, keeping his other hand in her mouth.

"Vine Girl!"

"Yes, mistress?"

"Bring me the Inside Out Man."

"Oh, no," she whines.

"Do it."

×

The sound of the Inside Out Man's feet as they approach M is like large, wet sponges slapping on the stones. M begins to scream. And scream. She may have seen her entire family slaughtered, she may have just been groped by a horny minotaur, but the Inside Out Man?

Not pretty.

And *awfully messy*.

"Get away from me!" She snarls and struggles, the slender little muscles standing out in her legs.

"Don't dislocate anything, dear. *Shhh*, gentle now," I say.

He wheezes, wetly.

She has not even seen him clearly yet, not with the flickering torches, but she can see enough to know she wants to see no more.

"Stay away. Don't come any closer," she wails. Then to me: "I'll take the bull man! I'll take the fucking bull man!"

Is it consent she is giving? Have I won? It's a gray area. I must *make sure* that she has just consented to her deflowering by Freight—but to take my threat far enough that she is not so *choosy*. You see, I'm beginning to think *I* would like that honor.

The cock that the Inside Out Man projects before him as he advances is a destroyed thing, a meaty, bloody, venous thing with all that should be inside, displayed outside. M's mouth becomes an open cavern when she sees it.

"Pleeeeeaaase," she pleads. The posts wobble with the force of her revulsion.

"Please what?"

She struggles.

"Please *what?*"

The Inside Out Man waits, leering through eyes that sag from their sockets.

"Fuck you!" she spits.

I pout. "That's not very creative. You already said that once."

The Inside Out Man leaves gory trails as he draws his upright torpedo of a cock along her belly, down past her hips. He hikes her shift up, revealing a small, fully-furred pussy. His dripping hand reaches for it.

She looks at me, her eyes big, all

fight gone.

"Please, I'll do anything you want."

×

(If you'll allow me another interruption: Often virgins expect their deflowering to occur in soft lighting, romantic circumstances. They expect verse, kind fingers, a formal recital of love. This is nonsense. A construct created out of whole cloth, so that humans are inevitably disappointed with their lives. What can be done? It's simple: Show them the other, darker possibilities to losing their coveted flower (rape by 60 winged gorillas, or the Inside Out Man, for one) and your virgin will be *very* appreciative of what he or she *does* get. Even *grateful*. You'll be on your way to a mutually beneficial deflowering in no time—and you won't have to use a single candle, rose petal, or maudlin love song.)

×

3: Positive Reinforcement

We are in a lavish bedroom with white silk bedspread and crimson swathes of curtains. A child-sized squirrel in emerald livery dozes on a silk chair in the corner, and oleander perfumes the air.

M is a tiny form in the center of the vast bed. Her damaged gown has been replaced with a gauzy nightgown of black, her legs encased in stockings like smoke. She blinks and rubs her forehead, a conical breast falling free of the garment.

"Where...am I? Who are *you*? Oh, my head."

"You're safe now," I coo.

She runs her fingers across her belly, up to her breasts, and across her smooth forehead. She is free of wounds. "I had a terrible dream."

"And now you are awake," I whisper. "Now you are safe."

She nods, dazed. "I remember a monster..."

"Forget that. You must rest."

She shakes her head and I am glad that she has no distinct memory of the Underworld— it doesn't always work so well, these transitions. But really, what she remembers does not matter now. For she has given <u>consent</u>. I conjure open the drapery. The suns are setting on the Realm. Fingers of mauve fall on us. The Mountains of Forgetfulness shine like black diamonds, and beyond, the Sky City blooms distant and vibrant in the early morning clouds. From here, all looks perfect.

I drift onto the bed and wrap my arms around her.

"There, there, it's over now. I won't let those people get you again."

"There was a woman," she says, shuddering. "An evil woman."

We sink to gather into pillows of ermine, satin and silk slipping beneath us. I nuzzle the line of her collarbone.

"She's gone now. And you, you are beautiful," I say.

I kiss her on the mouth and to my surprise I find her kissing *me*, pushing *me* back on the covers and holding me down with her mouth, soft and wet and warm. Her small hands find my breasts and in a moment she has freed them from my dress. For a long moment she looks at them, and then smiles at me before coming in for another deep kiss. Virgins do not often act so, do they?

"Stop," I say.

"Why?" she says. She is kissing my breasts now, trailing her kisses between the two as if she cannot decide which to kiss first.

"Because it is I who must lead you," I say. "You are a virgin."

She straddles me and laughs, throwing back her dark curls and looking down on me with mirth.

"I *am* a virgin," she says. "But perhaps I could teach you something as well? Perhaps I can help you be happy?"

Does she see my sadness?

"I *am* happy," I tell her.

She is a creature of fire and sugar. We roll together in a tumble of fabrics and naked parts, until she gets me under her control again—I let her, for I am curious—and she lowers herself between my spread legs.

"What shall I do first?" she says.

She licks her lips and traces one finger up my calf, beneath my knee, and up my inner thigh.

"You must first slow down," I whisper. The sunrise is coloring the room with a rosy, gauzy hue. "A lover must create anticipation."

"I don't want to slow down," she says. "Isn't youth supposed to be impetuous?"

She brings her lovely face closer to my cunt, bare and shining with arousal already. Her eyes are on it and she has a little smile.

"Shall I kiss it here first?" she kisses my labia.

I look up at the curtains swathing the bed and I gasp.

"No. Not there. Kiss my thighs first, one, two, three, all the way up. And grip me and stroke me with your fingers. Work your way up. Be smooth, playful, but be confident in everything you do."

She takes direction marvelously, her soft curls caressing my flesh as she kisses and nibbles her way to my nucleus.

"May I use my tongue?" she asks, applying her pointy little tongue as if in a mockery of how I used mine on her just an hour before. It presses against my still-hooded clitoris and it is as if she has blown a kiss on a dandelion—

seeds of pleasure explode out from that spot, filling my body. I arch my back and moan.

"Oh," I say, trying to calm myself. "Use your tongue, oh! Yes, that's right— but *gently* at first. Too fast and I'll become desensitized, little friend. Oh! Oh! Oh!"

She applies herself to her task until I am panting and tingling. My toes are trembling, my limbs splayed out as if I am tied to an invisible stanchion. Her tongue moves with quick precision up and down the length of my slit, drinking in my juices like a hungry kitten.

"Now, harder. And use your finger, but only gently."

"Yes, ma'am," she says. She inserts a finger, far too low, penetrating my anus, slicked from my fluttering cunt.

"Not there!" I cry, but I buck with

the lightning pleasure of it. How I wish to be filled and fucked!

She will not be stopped. With an imp's grin, her face wet with our lovemaking, she forces her finger into that narrower portal. I start to lose my composure, my control. I let a wave of pleasure break over me. When I have brought myself under control I think that I know what to do next. I feel her finger easing deeper, wrapped in my tighter passage. I stop her.

"You shouldn't have done that," I laugh.

Then, still pinned by her stubborn finger, I mockingly scold her.

"Poor marks for you, M, dear. Should I send you back to that awful nightmare woman?" I summon the liveried squirrel. "Stuart! Come, you lazy creature."

Stuart the squirrel wakes and stands

at attention in one fluid movement, whiskers trembling on his little nose.

"Yes, Queen. I was awaiting your pleasure, Queen."

There was a time when a servant would not dare to slumber on the job. But I am in a good mood and I don't obliterate him.

"The Rod, please, Stuart."

The Rod was carved from wood of the Sleeping Forest, and has been ingeniously affixed to a girdle of finest griffin leather so that it protrudes from one's belly when strapped over the hips.

M's eyes grow wide as she plucks it from the squirrel's golden tray. Stuart bows and slips away, tail twitching in discreet servant style.

"Do you know what I want you to do with that?"

M nods slowly. She studies its length in her hand and then kisses along the shaft, her eyes fastening on mine.

"Now, you must be *gentle*," I warn.

But she seems to have forgotten the lesson, for once she manages to fit its bulbous head inside of my cunt, she starts to push hard and deep. I cry out at the fullness of it, the ferocity of the little hand easing it deeper and deeper with each firm thrust. And then she pulls her trick again, pulling it out and pressing its moist tip into my asshole. I cry out with pain and pleasure. I grip the sheets and buck. The wrongness of it sends me over the edge.

"You have to take all of it," she says.

She is focused now, biting her glorious full lip, her breasts bouncing up and down and forward and back as she sways into me and away. The depth of it is unbearable and I come, and come and come, great tides of acute sensation carrying me away. I am hissing like a cat. I seem to rock in and out of existence, every inch of my body disappearing in importance, but for that radiating coal at my center.

After that, total collapse. Juddering breaths. Aftershocks of pleasure.

She is certainly an incredible human. Worthy of my husband. But he won't get her now. He'll realize what he has been doing.

And she? Well, she has brought me the pain I needed. I can think clearly. Stuart returns with water and wine, and we lie together, M and I, stroking each other's skin.

"Will you do me next?" she says,

snuggling into my side.

My dear, I want to say, that is the whole point. I will skewer her virginity on the Rod as soon as I recover.

"Thank you for the lesson, teacher."

×

I roll over, languidly reaching for M's sleek flank, her silken skin. But the sheets are empty. I reach farther. I grope for her, opening my eyes.

No.

I jump up on all fours and search the pillows. I fling pillows over my head, scattering the bedding around the room.

"No!" I cry.

No. No. No! And then I am tearing everything apart, ripping down the curtains, punching holes in the walls.

Stuart, cringing, dashing for the door, and I am screaming now, over and over, "*No.*"

×

No.

III

Overcoming Obstacles

"Where is she?" I shriek.

I tear through the Onyx Hall, fawning minions and hooded servants falling away on either side like leaves in a gale. "What have you done with her?"

My husband looks up from his cups, bleary eyed. Has he grown more decrepit? Has he already sated his ancient lust with M? With Peter? I point a quivering finger at him.

"You will destroy us all. With your selfish dalliances. A few were nothing, but now everything is…" I gesture to the fine dust that hangs in the air, the faint pall over everything. "Don't you feel it? How the realm slips with your waning love for me?"

The Onyx Hall has fallen into silence, the musicians having frozen mid-chord.

"Me?"

My king fairly creaks to his feet. The lines on his face deepen. He points back at me, fingers knobby as tree burls. The changelings weep above, dropping a rain of tears. Never before have I heard them weep.

"You are the one who has been sleeping with every goddamn being you can get your hands on," he bellows.

I stand, glowering at him. "Don't turn it around."

"I seek rejuvenation! You seek only revenge," he shouts, and has to lean on the table like an old man.

"See? Everything is falling apart. Even you. The Bog Mother warned I had to stop it. But you might as well know what you're doing to us," I say quietly. "It is *you*, always choosing your next conquest, leaving me to myself night after night, awaiting the night you will no longer come to our bed at all."

He looks steadily at me.

I conjure a wind that spins out of the north and through the Onyx Hall, tumbling the musicians and the lost babies and the courtiers and minions out the vast front doors, which slam shut.

"Forget the humans and help me

rebuild our realm," I whisper in the empty room.

My shoulders have crept up on either side of my neck like those of an infuriated cat, but my husband only laughs at my display. It is an earthy sound, as if reverberating through a deep cavern. I run from the Hall and through the moors to the borderlands where the Realm gives way to a sandy, bemisted void. It has grown wider, extending sandy fingers into the once-lush land. From within, the Bog Mother trudges toward me over the shifting sands. Her scent of growth and decay intensifies but she seems smaller somehow, less fertile.

"He will move on them tonight," she rasps. Her breathing is labored in the thin border air. "I passed a pack of his black dogs a quarter of an hour ago.

They are bound for the Real, where they are to coax the two lovelies to come to a certain place."

"Where?"

"The Carnival," she says.

I shudder. "Tell me what to do."

"You must go there. You must make an example of M and Peter for your people."

"I've been trying," I say.

She leans in to me and I can smell her foul breath.

"If you let him get away with this deliberate betrayal, this public defiance, it will surely destroy everything. Your people don't believe in your authority, and now they won't believe in him, either. Without belief all things will fade."

"Why *now*?"

Her eyes roll back. "Go and finish what you started. But it may already be too late."

"Has he gone mad? Why does he risk his destruction for lust?"

She only shivers. I turn and run faster than I have ever moved, across the barren borderlands to the place we call the Ruin Carnival.

×

1: Selecting Your Training Equipment

One problem with your world is that it's riddled with holes, weak patches as thin as ice, whole buildings and forests where reality is as porous as cheesecloth. While I prefer the sleeker, surer entry point offered by dreams, I can, when necessary, physically visit your world in certain places. The holes make this possible. We have ways of suggesting, by way of whispering at the edges of your subconscious minds, that you visit these places. Ever have a desperate desire to take the dusky path into the wet woods? To wander into a midnight cave? Climb to a creaking attic? That's us. Maybe a troll wants a better look at you. Or a mire witch needs a few of your human hairs for a spell.

The Ruin Carnival reads the dangling wooden sign in front. Deserted. Oh, it's a lovely disaster. Beyond its rusted gates lies the carnival with its ranks of rigged games, now silent and defunct, but still displaying shelf upon shelf of decrepit yet *living* prizes: Plush elephants swing rotting trunks, tin hyenas chuckle to themselves; jacks-in-the-box bounce lasciviously, tiny trains puff, motionless, beside rows of bears humming a ballad.

As you enter the Ruin Carnival you see a pond in which wooden ducklings romp atop other ducks in a clacking of beaks and private parts, sloshing the algae-choked waters. If you catch a ride through the Tunnel of Lust just beyond, you will see platinum milkmaids poled by pewter shepherds, brass dormice writhing in tinkling orgies — a clockwork bacchanal for your passing pleasure. Yet the *piece de resistance* of the Ruin Carnival is certainly the Crying Carousel.

It's not an ordinary carousel. Clockwork camels and bears with human hands and faces, giant swans and doves and mermaids and gorgons writhe and wriggle as it turns, wickedly that-way-going, not just round and round, but up and down, as arms and legs and necks and tiny wasp waists and breasts and hips and cocks plunge and press faster and faster and faster. The creatures trapped in service to the monstrous carousel make constant low-throated whines, moans, and cries of delight, but also, often, of despair.

It's *that* kind of carousel.

×

I arrive, having used all my powers to rush. The carnival is empty.

I have hardly a moment to push past the rusted front gate when who should come up the dirt road outside— the Real's only pathway to this lonely outpost between two worlds—but M and Peter. The Bog Mother was right: My husband's minions *have* been planning this, planting the suggestion that M and Peter come here. Clever king, but not as clever as I. Or as fast.

Peter is fresh-faced and floppy-haired in an aged sweatshirt and sneakers, casual for the day. M is harder in appearance—perhaps her nightmares have made her protective of her body, if not her mind. She wears a white-collared shirt and a black leather jacket, a slender pair of jeans and riding boots that gleam with buckles and straps. Her short hair is combed back behind her ears. They are each as marvelous in the Real as they are in mine.

M and Peter push open the gate, right on schedule, hand in hand and suitably impressed at the Ruin Carnival. I stay out of sight as they gaze around them and chatter in their native language about the strange, corrupt place they have discovered.

"I've got to bring my camera next time," says Peter, gazing at a collapsing Ferris wheel above their heads. "This place is a trip."

"How did you find it?" asks lovely little M, kicking aside an ancient Cracker Jack box. "It's got to be condemned, or something.

"Welcome to the carnival," I say, stepping out from behind a large, rusting cotton candy machine. It's metal bowl rings like a ceremonial gong as I brush past. I can never resist a good entrance.

They jump.

"I'm sorry. We're not supposed to be here, are we?" says Peter. M, wary of me, stands a little behind him, her thick-lashed eyes wide. They see a frumpy woman in too-short khakis, thick-soled shoes, an overlarge blue parka, and Coke-bottle glasses—no one to gaze at for long.

I reassure them, as I invite them farther into the grounds, all the while explaining that, yes, the carnival has been long abandoned but they are welcome to look around while I am here.

"I own the place. We're thinking of bulldozing it, so you might as well get a look around before it's gone."

For a while I let them poke around the stilled rides and peer into the dusty cases and jars in the abandoned Freak Show, all the while urging them deeper, toward the carousel.

Do I hear my husband's dogs baying in the distance? I must be running out of time.

"Perhaps you'd like to see the *carousel?*"

They look at me, these two pretty humans with their scarred and smoking interior worlds. Can they sense my hurry? I see only trust and curiosity on Peter's smooth face, but is there a certain slyness on M's?

"Sure," says Peter.

M shrugs.

I lead them to the carousel. They look at it with uncomprehending eyes, and while their attention is locked there, I go to work as only a queen can.

×

(Sometimes virgins must be forced just a bit. You cannot hurt them or violate their sexual parts—I don't mean anything gross or vulgar like that. I mean, you have to play with their heads. Make them spin a little, a bit like a carousel spins everything out of focus. You see, humans love to carry their pasts with them, no matter how deadly those pasts may be. They do. If you can force them to free themselves from these pasts for just a moment, to *play*, you can achieve great things in the seduction department.)

×

2: Transformation Training

Peter starts to shout.

"What's happening?" he cries in a stilted voice.

"What the fuck is going on?" croaks M.

"Shhh," I say, and as I stump toward them I drop the frumpy look and take on my full form, though nude: my eyes full of wicked, sparkling shards of light, my limbs long, gleaming, my crowned head reaching above even Peter's, my many-hued hair cascading to form a scintillatingly modest cover for my breasts, my hips. "You ask what's happening. You are frozen and there is nothing you can do about it. I will not hurt you, but you must not struggle. You might even," I send my tongue like a flower stamen questing toward Peter's cheek and then withdraw it, "enjoy yourselves."

Yes, I have frozen them, as you might freeze someone by stopping time. Actually, I have made them *think* they are frozen—somewhat like those lewd, stilled figures on the carousel behind them.

We three are alone before the carousel and they are at my mercy. Shall I lay them down and press my cunt against their helpless lips? Shall I slide my tongue deep into Peter until he jets his virginal semen into the air? Shall I force M into a shuddering release that will make her weep? Tears come to my eyes—tears of anticipation and joy. I've got them now. My fingers tingle, my cunt is tensing with longing. I exhale, my mouth open, and walk to M. Her eyes follow me as I approach. I touch her long, dark hair, I soothe her while she shivers. I trace one hand between her breasts and unsnap the button of her jeans.

Peter can only regard me with big eyes, a subtle tremor at his throat where the blood flows.

Directly in front of M's watering eyes a donkey is on the brink of servicing a fairy-tale princess with his sizable tin part. Peter is motionless, facing a leering woodsman with a wood nymph of uncommon capacity poised above him, ready to take him in.

"Don't panic," I say. I place a calming spell on each of them. "Being frozen isn't so bad. Can't you feel the *freedom* there is in restraint? Is your little pussy not quivering in anticipation of what is coming, dear M? Is your thick cock not growing, Peter?" I can *sense* their arousal. It is gratifying, how predictable even stubborn, hipster virgins can be. "Relax into it. There are advantages. Pretend you are clockwork, like those on the carousel. Clockwork doesn't feel pain. Clockwork doesn't feel loss. And clockwork doesn't make war or weapons. Free yourself to simply *be*. And then you will be able to *play*."

The baying of hounds breaks the stillness of the carnival.

"We haven't much time," I say, "or I'd draw this out a little more. But you've given your consent, so now no more ceremony is necessary."

I flick a switch and the carousel begins to ease around. The hips and thighs and buttocks of its occupants shine like precious metal. With the first revolution the figures begin to move, up and down and back and forth. They wind and bounce, rutting and bumping, *this* going into *that* and *that* going into *this*, metal lips kissing metal lips above and below. Pistons swing and plunge and steam hisses and mirrors flash. The racket is deafening. Will it vibrate itself to pieces?

Unable to act, to defend themselves

or even to participate, M and Peter can, perhaps, leave their human suffering behind. This is the problem with humans. You have the tools to get over the horrors you inflict on one another, and yet you deliberately do not use them. You handicap yourself with honor and shame and this desire to remember those who died, so you can't get on with your own lives. *Love*, you call it. Centaur-shit, I call it.

I take Peter. Carefully I slide off the sweatshirt, remove the sneakers one-by-one, the jeans, until he is standing naked in all his athlete's glory, his skin flawless as a statue's. I have made him forget the cool air. He is breathing heavily, his cock having sprung to fullness already. The erotic carousel turns and turns, its whirring rhythm forming a strange sound track.

"Like clockwork," I say, gripping him.

Peter moans. I feel the pulse at the base of his cock. I press my other hand to my own pulse, my clitoris so ready that I have to squeeze my legs together and moan. I fix him with my eyes. I am beautiful. I am whatever he thinks is most beautiful. My breasts are hot against his chest, my nipples tingling against his.

"You're just a young man. You're not supposed to cry all the time. You're supposed to *play*."

He nods and I allow the motion. Beside him M gazes at us. I do hear the squeak of the rusted gate.

"I'm sorry about this," I say, and I turn, spreading my skirts to either side. I push back against his rigid cock.

"Say *please*."

"Please," croaks Peter, behind me. I relax my grip on his body and his arms come to gently tug my hair as I push back against him, absorbing him into my tight, hot interior.

He is of perfect proportion and he slides into me easily. The machine whirs, the mechanical lovers circle. I am pinned upon his thickness and I force myself back onto him until he is fully within me. I feel his hands on my hips, and he pulls me against him and holds me so that I cannot pull away. Instead he grinds his hips and drives his cock into my wetness, and I rock back and forth with him, little fires burning in each of my cells, the sharpness of pleasure growing. I think for a moment of my husband, how he used to take me this way, to draw my quaking body to his and hold me against him, something loved and cherished and fucked. I cry out and move my hips faster. The carousel flashes by.

Peter cries out and presses his head between my shoulders, probing me deeper and deeper. He grabs for my arms, pinning them on either side of my body as he starts to pump faster. Then, as he seems about to come, he slows down, reaches around to stroke my breasts. His fingers are soft and searching. I feel them circling my nipples, pinching, weighing, massaging, and I start to forget myself. I shift my ass around, getting the most of him in my cunt.

He kneads my breasts with a fierce urgency. I would exalt if he were not clinging so hard, if his strong young manhood hadn't transfixed me utterly, if sadness for my husband were not clouding my pleasure. And then *the moment* starts to come, unstoppable as a runaway train. I cannot help myself— the convulsions that originate low in my cunt begin to flutter out.

"Oh, Peter!"

My orgasm flows through him and takes him with it: He starts to gasp and cry out and then I feel his hot seed within me, a geyser of heat and sweetness deep within. I laugh. So long coming, this seed, and it is mine. I am victorious.

My husband must be very near. There is no time. I force M to the ground. I drag her legs up. Her clothes come away easily. My own wetness, and Peter's, courses down the inside of my thighs. I wrench her lovely legs over my shoulders, leaving only her head and shoulders on the grass, her arms dangling at her sides. I see a strange look in her eye, something knowing, something hard, something challenging and inviting all at once. Something that says, "I've been waiting." And then it is gone. Did I imagine it?

"I'm sorry, my pretty," I say brusquely, "but in a way you did agree to this." And there is no more talking. I send my questing tongue down between her breasts, trailing along the tiny pinkish-brown nipples, circling one and then the other as M's eyes roll back in her head, and then, I strike.

I find the tiny slip of her hymen with the tip of my tongue. I probe it. She gasps. I withdraw and circle her clitoris until I feel her breath growing more and more urgent. Peter, sated, no longer frozen, takes her hand. I wait until her breaths are coming in short pants, as if she is about to pass out, and then I thrust my tongue forward, through the flimsy barrier and deep into her interior.

Blood.

Puncturing that little scrap of flesh is the best thing I've done in years. Not so good for her: She screams. I give no quarter. I am angry, full of spite and sadness and I make sure she feels every bit of that as I slip my thick, long, killing tongue in and out of the briny passage.

"Stop," she pleads, but she cannot fight.

At last she relaxes and starts to squirm and shudder, the little slut, but she is a woman, after all. She squeals, trembles, and subsides. All the while the whirring of the carousel continues, the tinkling inanity of its carnival tune an appropriate accompaniment. For this is madness. And now the dogs are here, flooding through the carnival gates, around the exhibits, the tents, surrounding the carousel.

But they are too late. It is done. I am overcome with the ugliness of my reign, with weariness at existence. I am so tired. I look at their gleaming bodies and I vomit forth a wild sound.

My king gallops up on a centaur and slides to the ground in a jingling of buckles. He stands looking at me, his chest heaving.

"I am the Queen. I am the Queen. I AM THE QUEEN!" I shout at him. I drop M's legs and she slumps on the grass, a beautiful doll.

And no one can take my king

from me. Even if he is a cheating ass.

×

But this can't be right. My king is *smiling* at me. *Warmly*.

"Did you enjoy my little gift?" he says.

Is that a snicker he is holding back?

"*Your* gift?" I spit. "*Your* gift?"

He crosses his arms and leans against a waiting centaur, his antlers casting a strange shadow across the lawn. His black dogs mill about, sniffing.

"What?" I say. "What is going on?"

I look away, down at my conquests, only to find Freight and the vine girl gazing up at me, slick with sex, slightly transparent from the strain of being in the Real. The vine girl shrugs.

"We were following orders," she whispers.

My hands go to my hair and I pull at it, great clumps of it coming out. I want to destroy everything. It cannot be. *It cannot.*

"No," I say. "*You bastard.*"

IV

Knowing When
to Quit

They laugh. How they laugh. And so I am a joke in the end as in the beginning. After all, the humans evaded me, my husband outsmarted me, and my own faithful servants proved to be traitors.

The carousel is groaning to a stop: Someone has turned it off and its decrepit screeching dwindles and finally ends. We are left in silence, but for snorts of derision.

"You thought you could outwit me?" says my husband.

I can only shake my head, though I want to kill him. My eyes fall on my treacherous minions. Deaf to his screams, I grip Freight's head in my hands and I tear it away from his body. The vine girl's death is slower—I smash her flawless face into her skull until it is a pulpy mass of blood and shivering foliage. She wheezes and whines. Recovered somewhat, I turn to my master and king.

"It was *innocent* fun. And you do it too," he laughs.

The vine girl's piteous howls stop as she dies.

Now his eyes harden and his laugh turns to a sneer as he scans the bloody floor. "What little fun there is for an immortal who can no longer enjoy anything, who has seen everything, done everything. I am stagnating. You are stagnating. *That* is the true reason the Realm disintegrates brick by brick. Yet you think you should take pleasure away from me in our final days? My one lasting pleasure?"

I look at my hands, how they are riddled with veins. The Ruin Carnival dissolves and we are standing in the Onyx Hall. A cornice collapses and shatters on the stones, scattering the few servants who have dared return.

×

Things slip away for a time.

×

When I awake I am half sunk into the earth. Sickly green mists drift over my half unmade kingdom. I trail my fingers in stagnant water. There is nothing left to save, and if there were, why would I? My king has betrayed me over and over. I swish the waters angrily, and a fish, conjured by the fury, flashes into existence and out again. So I do still have some power.

After what may be an eternity I drag myself through the mud and onto a hillock. Far in the distance, through the fog and the landscape of my fading world, stand the Castle, its Onyx Hall, and my king. It is all nearly lost in a biting, alkaline fog.

I find him alone on his sunken throne, gazing into a goblet. It is empty and cracked. His antlers are draped in cobwebs. The Baby Garden is visible through the window, and it gives off a potent scent of putrefaction.

"You know, it seems funny now," he says, gazing past me, "how far all this went. But I never wanted to hurt you. I never wanted to hurt the Realm. I only wanted a bit of...freshness."

I find my way among the broken tiles to the smaller throne beside him. When I lower myself into it, dried mud breaks and scatters. I look at my grizzled love. Dust gauzes the banquet table. The marble columns, once bright, are now shattered and dull.

"I love you," he says.

"I could kill *you*," I say. "And where are all the courtiers?"

He peers off into the darkness beyond the Hall.

"We can make more," he says.

Just then a black dog trots up to my king. I stiffen at the sight of it, but it does not whisper in his ear. Instead it stands between us and plainly announces, "There's something you might want to see."

×

We follow the dog out of the Onyx Hall and over the moors and through the windswept borderland, back through the Ruin Carnival, its shoddy path, and eventually out onto a city street. We walk slowly, for we are no longer strong. We lean on one another, we two old, decrepit lovers. I no longer have the energy to kill him. My hair falls in grey curls around my shoulders.

The dog leads us to an old brownstone building on a quiet side street. The cars pass and the human children throw balls and a mailman drops mail into a chipped mailbox. No one glances up at two half-people with horns and talons and yellowing teeth.

"Did you stop loving me?" I say. "It's

all right to tell me. I'm not going to kill you anymore."

"I never did stop loving you. I stopped loving myself. The Realm. The Castle. The singing. The dancing. All of it. I was struggling to find something *new*. The callow joy of youth."

"A king is never satisfied that his kingdom is enough," I say to myself. Then to him: "Why couldn't you *share*? You think I don't want what's fresh, what's new?"

He shoots me a sly glance.

"You *did* look like you enjoyed seducing those two," he says shyly.

"Not a bit," I lie.

"Just lying back and thinking of the Realm, eh?"

"Don't make me take back what I said about killing you."

1: Success

We follow the dog up a complaining staircase. He stops and sits patiently outside a door marked 5. My husband turns the knob and we enter a small, beige box of an apartment. M's apartment. She lives here with her sadness, her virginity. And Peter is here, too. I gasp. My husband's mouth moves but no sound comes out.

You see, they are making love.

Imagine your first time. The only one you ever had; the only one you will ever have. It happened. It is gone. Or it will happen and you will then lose it forever. Awkward. Sticky. Anxious. Foggy, even. Or a thing of monumental beauty, as temporary and fragile as youth itself. This first time, whatever it is for *you* , is something my king and I will never have. Not like you. Though we may change ourselves to be young forever, we can never truly possess youth. And we can therefore never lose it.

This is an unspeakable sadness.

My husband and I stare open-mouthed at the beauty of these two youths caught in the throes of their own fledgling passion. It is all the stronger for their past pain, their loss, the terror of their younger days, and the repression they have inflicted on themselves to survive that agony.

I am reminded that the Realm exists because of humans—because of Man and his endless passions, his endless guilt and hang-ups and nightmares, his avoidances, his approaches, his terrible, silly failures, and his grandest achievements. Man is a visionary because he must age and die.

Seeing M and Peter—gentle, awkward, sighing—something breaks in us. I feel it in my king as strongly as in myself, for we are connected as tree trunks with their roots. Together my faded king and I weep.

M and Peter have found something physical to save them, and they cling to it, to each other. They have connected as I knew they must, someday. Together they can weather their nightmares, build new dreamscapes where mothers do not die at the end of soldiers' weapons, where children grow up happy. A dreamscape much like my Realm—but one from which they can come home every morning, and to which they may return every night.

Before us are the naked Man and Woman, ultimately rendered by life, youth, and yes, by the prospect of death. They are the perfect man and woman of whom we are only shadows, my immortal king and I.

There is no glamour in it: The light isn't perfect, there is no soothing music, the sheets are rough and cheap, the floors are gritty, cold. M has a small patch of dry skin on her shoulder. Peter has dark circles beneath his brooding eyes. My husband and I join hands and watch. How can we resist?

×

2: Letting Your Virgin Go

His hands catch in her tangled hair and M winces. She wishes she had brushed it better. He apologizes and feels brutish, overlarge. Still, none of these hiccups affect their passion. They keep going, scraping their skin across each other as if they would exchange pelts.

They are determined to do this.

×

Why now? Is it because I opened the

way, one small mythical queen from an adjacent realm? Or is it just time? Peter has learned a thing or two, though. I can't deny that.

×

Peter kisses her breasts, takes a fine nipple into his mouth, suckling. He would drink her if he could, he thinks. And then onto the next. His bites again, she closes her eyes in the agony of it, but the pressure and pleasure building throughout her body is palpable. The force of desire is unstoppable as she caresses his head, pulling him into her. Then he is kissing downward, across her taut stomach, the bellybutton a depression meant to be filled with kisses, the untrimmed brush of her pubic hair.

She becomes very still when he kisses beneath her bellybutton, frozen like a deer in a pasture. He finds the tiny nub at the center and he kisses and nuzzles it. She worries that she smells all right and tenses. But gradually she unfreezes and guides his head so that his tongue and lips are where she likes it best. She sighs and closes her eyes.

×

I elbow my king.

"I taught her that," I say.

×

Peter obeys M's guidance, moving his tongue in a series of licks and deep kisses that sends her singing in a high-pitched solo that in turn sets Peter's heart thumping. His chest throbs. His manhood, already aching with lust, grows between his legs. He wants to bury it inside her heat, to feel the hairs tickle his belly.

×

I taught him this too. But I do not say it out loud. My husband is absorbed in the show, but as if reading my mind he says, "You always were a good instructor."

I squeeze his big hand, feeling a little sheepish. My king seems stronger now, as if the apartment's close air is nourishing him. He looks straighter, less stooped, and his eyes glint in the old way, as if shards of crystal are lodged within. He's a lecher, this one, but he is mine. That much is clear to me now.

×

M feels the pinnacle of pleasure approaching, just as she felt it in her dreams, and in those few moments she has touched herself. But before the moment takes her she pushes Peter from between her legs. His hair a mess, he looks hurt until she reaches to caress his cock and testicles. Gently.

×

"I didn't teach her that!" I cry in pleasure.

My husband looks slyly at me and I punch him in the arm.

×

Now Peter is kissing M deeply to show he is grateful for her attentions. He is fully hard and worries he will explode if he does not enter her. He sees that she wants it too, how can she not, and he starts to guide his slick head into her small, furry slit. They laugh when it is not the right angle, when it will not go past her labia. Instead he settles beside her and she turns to face him and they kiss for a few minutes. And then, awkwardness forgotten, he slides atop her again, and enters her heat, this time the right way. This time the way is smooth and he pushes slowly against her natural tightness. Gradually he moves deeper.

And cries out her name.

"Please, I want to…" he says, but cannot finish the sentence, cannot be so crude, not with her. "I want to…".

"Fuck me. I want you to fuck me, Peter," *she says, looking up at him, nodding for him to go on. She flexes her little muscles and squeezes him encouragingly. "It's okay to say it."*

Then she gives a little gasp as he breaks her hymen.

"Oh, it hurts."

"Are you okay?" he asks. "I didn't know…"

"I'm okay," she says, laughing a little, a tear leaking out of one eye. "It didn't even hurt that bad."

"I'm sorry," he says, smoothing her hair.

But she is already pushing her hips up in welcome. When he is seated deeply inside of her he nearly comes.

And then they fall into a rhythm and they are one.

×

We retreat down the stairs of the old apartment building, silent and thoughtful. They have survived us, M and Peter, and they have survived the Real, at least so far.

And what of me? What of my husband? What of us? He hulks beside me, an enormous weight who makes the very floors creak. Though we are shadows of what we once were, we can rebuild. And as to betrayal? Well, it goes both ways with our kind, doesn't it? One thing is clear: We deserve each other. And we, unlike the two loving humans behind us, are made of the very same stuff. Hard stuff. He is I and I am he.

It's a bitter thing, discovering how things are, discovering that what is lost can never be recovered. I suppose my king and I will tuck our tails under and go back to our realm. Maybe we will rebuild it in a new way, one more exciting to us...at least for a few hundred more years, and then boredom will surely set in again. Eternal life does not promise variety, you know. Perhaps we will close the pathways behind us this time—knock down the Ruin Carnival and hide the other weak spots, leave the humans to their dreams. Fade into the background for a millennium or so.

Immortality is a farce, you see. A movie that is good at first but sends you fleeing in boredom halfway in, only to discover there's no exit—it's an eternal second reel. And anyway, your kind doesn't need our kind, does it? We're the ones who needed yours. But we'll withdraw for now.

We shuffle out of your world, saying goodbye to the Real, maybe forever.

×

Well, *almost* goodbye. We go, but not before snagging a few willing hussies from the Catholic school down the block. We *do* like virgins, you know.

THE END

ABOUT THE AUTHOR

Wednesday Black is a writer of fiction, nonfiction, and poetry. She studied writing at the University of Michigan in Ann Arbor, Michigan, where she spent part of her childhood, and at The New School in New York City. She splits her time between New York and New Orleans. This is her first work of erotic fiction.